DONNY
GETS A SHOT

A boy is taken by his Mommy to the doctor to get a shot

Donny Gets A Shot / Donald L. Straub

Story summary: Donny Gets A Shot is a book about a young boy whose mom takes him to the doctor to get a shot but as you will see he really does not want to get it. Watch how mom and the nurse handle the situation.

Dedication

This book is dedicated to my wife, Margaret. She has accepted me and allowed me to do as I wish, in pursuit of becoming who I was meant to be.

DONNY
GETS A SHOT

A boy is taken by his Mommy to the doctor to get a shot

"Good morning, Donny! It's time to get up!"
Mommy said from my bedroom doorway as she poked her
head in.

"Mmmuhhh...morning Mommy!"
I said somewhat reluctantly as I was just waking up.

"Are you ready for breakfast?"
Mommy asked in an upbeat tone.

"Yes please! I'm so-o-o-o hungry!"
I said as I was rubbing the sleep from my eyes.

"What would you like for breakfast? You can have anything you want this morning! Today's a "**special day**", Mommy said once again in an upbeat tone.

"Pancakes would be great! May I please have pancakes this morning?" I said in the same happy tone as Mommy. "Is Daddy home?"

"Sure! I will make you pancakes for breakfast. No, Dad already went to work. Go ahead and get dressed and then come downstairs for breakfast. I will start the pancakes now so don't take too long," Mommy said.

"Okay!" I got dressed putting on my favorite shirt. With my socks and shoes in my hand I walked down the stairs to the kitchen where mommy was making breakfast. We always ate breakfast in the kitchen.

I spread some butter on my pancakes and Mommy poured some syrup on top of them for me. I always like thick pancakes so the syrup soaks in to them. Mommy poured a nice glass of orange juice for me to drink.

As I was eating my pancakes I asked, "What are we going to do today, Mommy? Are we going to the zoo? I love the zoo. I love all the animals. You said this was a **"special day"**.

What my mommy said next brought sheer panic and fear to me. I couldn't believe she thought this was going to be a **"Special Day!"** "We're going to go see the doctor today!" Mommy said almost excitedly.

"Oh it won't be that bad!" Mommy said holding back a chuckle. "You will see! Bring me your socks and shoes so we can put them on. After your shoes are on you can go brush your teeth and finish getting ready."

I stomped my feet as I took the unbearably long walk upstairs to my bedroom to finish getting ready. I brushed my teeth for an extra long time and washed my hands really, really well, trying to take as much time as possible.

I slowly made the long, long walk down the stairs stomping my feet every step of the way. This was the longest hike I ever made down those too familiar stairs to meet Mommy at the front door of our house.

Mommy helped me get in my car seat in the backseat of mommy's car. She drove us straight to the doctor's office. She was softly singing and humming the entire trip. I think she was trying to get my mind off "the grizzly event" that was about to occur.

Mommy got out of the car and then helped me out of the car. I stood with my head hung low. I was sniffling with tears in my eyes and shuffling my feet every step of the way.

Mommy took my hand in her hand and we walked into the doctor's office. I was walking as slowly as Mommy would let me walk, shuffling and dragging my feet with my head hung low.

As we stood in the doctor's office I was clinging tightly to mommy's leg with my eyes full of tears and I began to sniffle.

Mommy told me to go over to the play area of the waiting room. Mommy talked to the lady at the window of the doctor's office and did some stuff with her.

When mommy finished with the lady at the window, Mommy sat in one of the chairs in the waiting area reading a magazine. I continued to look at the toys not really playing with any of them. Now more tears were forming in my eyes and beginning to trickle down my cheeks.

After a few minutes we were called in to the doctor's office. With my head hung low Mommy took me by my hand again and walked me down the exceptionally long, long hall into the tiny room.
This was the longest walk of my life.

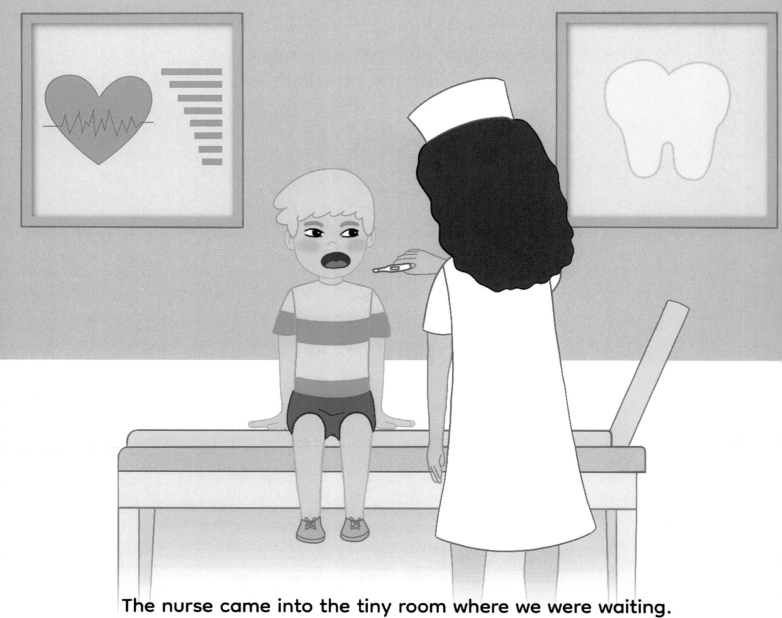

The nurse came into the tiny room where we were waiting. She put this thing in my ear so she could take my temperature. "That's 98.6!" she said. My temperature was perfect. She then said she would be giving me **"the shot"**.

I looked at my mommy. My eyes got wide, filling with tears and I shouted **"NO! This is going to hurt!"** The tears were now beginning to stream from my eyes down my cheeks once again.

My mommy did her best to calm me down while the nurse was getting the shot ready.

I continued to tear up and began to cry calling out loudly,
"NO!!! NO!!! NO!!!... Mommmmy!!!"

The nurse just came up quietly behind me, took hold of my arm, and gently slipped the needle into my arm.

"All done! That's it! It's all over!" the nurse said calmly and quietly to my mommy. She carefully put a small bandage that had different colored dots on it over the teeny, tiny hole in my arm from the shot.

"What...? It's over? It's all over? But I didn't feel anything! I didn't bleed to death or anything!", I said as I was fighting back the sniffling from all the earlier crying. Mommy pulled a tissue from her purse and sweetly wiped the tears from my eyes and let me blow my nose.

"Lets go home now!" Mommy said in her calmest most reassuring manner.

As we are starting to walk away from the doctor's office I say "Good bye!" to the nice nurse. I had the tiniest hint of a smile starting to form on my face.

We both got in the car and Mommy started to drive us home.

On our way home mommy surprised me. She stopped and got me a single scoop of mint chocolate chip ice cream in a sugar cone from the store. It looked like it was going to be a pretty good day after all.